7-2022

Paul Bunyan

AND BABE THE BLUE OX

As told by
DAPHNE HOGSTROM

Illustrated by
ART SEIDEN

D1196706

WHITMAN PUBLISHING DIVISION
Western Publishing Company, Inc.   Racine, Wisconsin
© 1967 by Western Publishing Company, Inc.
Produced in the U.S.A.

Paul Bunyan was a mighty man,
A GIANT man was he.
He was the greatest lumberjack
Who ever chopped a tree.
As tall as twenty buildings!
As strong as twenty bears!
As brave as twenty lions!
As swift as twenty hares!

He used a broadax and a saw
To comb his inky locks.
And almost just as large as he

Was Babe, his big blue ox!

Now Babe—colored a shining blue,
Like sunny summer sky—
Was as wide as the Missouri
And eleven pine trees high!

Old Jim the crow (or so they say)
Would fly from horn to horn.
He'd leave one wintry evening —

To arrive one summer's morn!

No one can tell how Babe was found,
Though many songs are sung
Of how Babe wandered into camp
When he was very young.
Paul Bunyan raised and trained his pet
To carry, pull, and pack.
And Babe would feel rewarded
By a pat upon his back.

But others say that Babe was found
The year the blue snow fell.
It covered tracks and trails and trees
And Babe the Ox, as well.
His tail, they claim, was poking out
From snowdrifts on the rocks.
And when Paul Bunyan pulled on it —

He pulled out Babe the Ox!

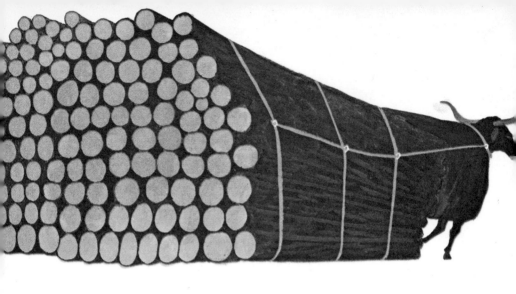

Babe did the job of sixty men
Around that camping ground.
He'd haul five hundred logs at once —
And pile them in a mound.

He dragged whole forests to the shore.
He straightened crooked roads.
He packed whole camps upon his back.
He towed GIGANTIC loads!

The loggers tell about his deeds
Around their fires at night.
They tell of how he'd strive and strain
And work with all his might.
They say he could pull anything,
A mountain or a log.
But would you think that even Babe
Could ever pull a FOG?

One winter's day,
  a fog lay thick
On Paul's huge
  lumber camp.
It made the woods
  grow deep and dark
With icy cold
  and damp.

The river fishes lost their way
And swam up in the air,
Till even Paul himself could brush
The salmon from his hair!
The little Giddy Fish got caught
Among the limbs of trees.
And there they tried to swish and swim,
As happy as you please.

But Paul and Babe plowed ditches
In the river's crimson clay.

Then both together tugged and lugged—
And drained that fog away!

They say that Babe pulled rivers, too —
Long curly, twirly rills
That gave the loggers extra work
When floating logs to mills.

Old Paul would hitch him to a wave.
Then Babe would huff and puff
Until his master cried out, "Stop!
That stream is straight enough!"

But sometimes Babe was troublesome,
As when he tried to tub.
He'd need at least a little *lake*
In which to scour and scrub,

And *tons* and *tons* of yellow soap,
And *barrelfuls* of cream —
But when the job was finished
How he'd shimmer, shine, and gleam!

Then, feeding Babe could be a task.
His mouth held *bales* of hay.
And often, as you might expect,
The wire got in his way.

So while he chewed, and chawed, and
    chomped,
Ten strong men stood beneath
With pitchforks in their hands to pick
The wire between his teeth!

Now, Babe was just one hundred
When his strength began to fail.
He found it hard to haul a house,
Or straighten out a trail.

Paul put him in a pasture
On the very edge of town,
Where he could see the people pass
As they rode up and down.

And Babe was very happy,
For the children came in flocks
To climb the tail and pat the back of
BABE, THE BIG BLUE OX!